Meredith Hooper

was born in Australia, and travelled on a scholarship
to do post-graduate study at Nuffield College, Oxford. An historian by training,
she is a Visiting Research Fellow in the History of Science at the Royal Institution,
and a member of the Association of British Science Writers.
She specialises in writing on Antarctica. She has travelled to the continent
on three occasions to work on Antarctic stations as a writer. She has been awarded
the Antarctica Medal by the US Congress and is currently a Visiting Scholar
at the Scott Polar Research Institute in Cambridge.
Her books for Frances Lincoln include *Antarctic Journal*, *Ice Trap!*,
The Island that Moved, *The Pebble in my Pocket* and
The Drop in my Drink.

Bert Kitchen

was born in Liverpool and studied textile design,
drawing and painting at the Central School of Art in London. He is now
a full-time author and illustrator of children's books.
His best-known titles include *Animal Alphabet* (Puffin)
and the Animal Lives series (Kingfisher).

First published in Great Britain under the title *Tom's Rabbit*
in 1998 by Frances Lincoln Children's Books, 4 Torriano Mews,
Torriano Avenue, London NW5 2RZ

www.franceslincoln.com

First paperback edition published in 1999

The author and publishers would like to thank Robert K. Headland,
Archivist and Curator of the Scott Polar Research Institute, for his help.

British Library Cataloguing in Publication Data available on request

ISBN 1-84507-393-2

Set in Perpetua

Printed in China

9 8 7 6 5 4 3 2 1

*The book is dedicated to the work
of the Antarctic Heritage Trust*

Tom Crean's Rabbit

A True Story from Scott's Last Voyage

Meredith Hooper

Illustrated by Bert Kitchen

FRANCES LINCOLN CHILDREN'S BOOKS

The story in this book really happened, on a voyage
to Antarctica in 1910. The ship was called the Terra Nova.
Her captain was Robert Scott, and Tom Crean,
the sailor, was a member of the crew.

Tom the Sailor picked up Little Rabbit carefully in his big hands. He wrapped her in an old woolly jumper.

"You need a nest, Little Rabbit," said Tom. "Somewhere on this ship there is just the right place — warm and quiet and cosy. Let's go and find it."

Tom the Sailor looked at the black cat with one white whisker. The ship's cat was tucked up in a warm, cosy place. He lay in his own little hammock, just like the sailors' hammocks, with his own little pillow and blanket.

"This hammock is full of black cat," said Tom. "There's no room for you here, Little Rabbit."

Tom the Sailor looked up at the skylight where the ship's parrot was swinging on her perch.

"Hallo, Polly," said Tom.

"Hallo, Polly," said the parrot.

"You can't live on a perch, Little Rabbit," said Tom, and gave the parrot a piece of string to unravel.

Carefully Tom the Sailor climbed down the ladder into the ship's hold. There were boxes and sacks and barrels, in stacks and heaps. It was very cold.

Tom peered around and shivered. "It's much too cold and dark down here for you, Little Rabbit," he said, and climbed back up again quickly.

Tom the Sailor looked into the big cabin. Everyone was busy hanging up paper lanterns, paper chains and flags.

"Come and help us put up the decorations!" they called. "Come on, Tom."

"Not now," said Tom. "I have to find a nest for my rabbit."

Good smells were coming from the galley. Tom looked around the door. The cook was stirring something in a big saucepan.

"What's for dinner?" asked Tom.

"Special surprises for a special dinner," said the cook. "You just wait and see."

Tom the Sailor put on his big, warm jacket. He pulled on his woolly hat and woolly gloves.

"We're going up on deck, Little Rabbit," said Tom. "Mind now, keep warm!"

Snow was falling gently. The sea was covered in big pieces of ice like white meringue. Icebergs floated slowly by, like spiky mountains.

Two whales lifted their great backs in a patch of blue-black water, then sank below the surface.

Fat, silvery seals lay on the ice, yawning and scratching themselves with their flippers. A little group of penguins stood staring at the ship. More penguins scurried across the ice in a long line. One penguin climbed to the top of an ice hill and the others pushed him off.

High above the deck, up against the sky, a wooden barrel was lashed to the mast. Pure white birds flew round and round the rigging.

"It's no good going up there with you, Little Rabbit," said Tom. "You can't climb, and you can't fly."

The deck was filled with dogs. Brown dogs, hairy dogs, black and yellow dogs with pointy ears and curly tails.

Tom tucked Little Rabbit deep inside his jacket.

"Hallo, dogs!" said Tom. The dogs barked and yelped and howled.

Tom the Sailor went forward to the place where the
ponies were kept in strong wooden stalls. The ponies were
munching oats. They banged at the sides of their stalls with
their sharp hooves.

"This ship is full up," said Tom, "it's crammed and
crowded. Where can I find you a warm, quiet, cosy place
for your nest, Little Rabbit?"

Little Rabbit's long, silky ears drooped.

"I've got it!" shouted Tom suddenly. He ran down eight steps, and poked his head into a gap under the deck where the hay for the ponies was stored. The air smelt sweet.

"Just the place for a nest!" said Tom. Carefully he unwrapped Little Rabbit from the old woolly jumper, and put her on to the hay. Little Rabbit hopped around, sniffed the hay, and lay down.

"And now," said Tom happily, "it's time for my Christmas dinner!"

Everyone sat down around the long table in the big cabin.
They ate . . .

Tomato Soup

Roast Mutton

Plum Pudding

Mince Pies

Then they opened little parcels from their families.
They pulled crackers, and played games, and sang songs.
They were a very long way away from home, but it was
a good Christmas party.

When it was nearly bedtime, Tom went to see if Little Rabbit was all right.

He poked his head into the gap under the deck where the hay was stored. Little Rabbit lay in her warm, cosy nest in the hay. Lying next to her were seventeen baby rabbits.

"That's the best Christmas present ever!" said Tom, happily. "Seventeen babies! Now I can give a rabbit to each of my friends. Well, nearly!"

And he stroked Little Rabbit's long, silky ears.

Tom looked around at the night. The deck was covered
in glittering snow. The world was utterly quiet and still.
The sun was a soft golden ball, and the ice glowed white,
with purple shadows.

"Happy Christmas," said Tom to the world.

The great white continent of Antarctica is surrounded by ice-covered seas.
On Christmas Day, 1910, the Terra Nova was pushing through the ice, towards
land. The men on board, led by Captain Scott, hoped to be the first people to
reach the South Pole. Their husky dogs and ponies would help pull sledges loaded
with food, tents and sleeping bags across the frozen snow.

Tom Crean got close to the South Pole before turning back and helping to save
the life of another explorer. Captain Scott, with four companions, did reach
the Pole, only to find that a Norwegian expedition led by Roald Amundsen had
arrived before them. Scott and his companions died on the return journey.

Tom Crean had many adventures in Antarctica. Along with the explorer, Sir Ernest Shackleton, he sailed a tiny boat across the wild ocean, after the ship Endurance had been crushed in the ice. Later he went back home to Ireland, and ran the South Pole Inn.

The story of Tom's rabbit is based on diaries kept by men on the Terra Nova. Scott wrote in his diary, "An event of Christmas was the production of a family by Crean's rabbit. She gave birth to 17… at present they are warm and snug…"

Meredith Hooper's descriptions of Antarctica are inspired by her travels as a writer with the Australian National Antarctic Research Expedition.

MORE PICTURE BOOKS BY MEREDITH HOOPER FROM FRANCES LINCOLN

Ponko and the South Pole

In Association with the National Maritime Museum, Greenwich
Illustrated by Jan Ormerod

Ponko the Penguin and his friend, Joey Bear, like adventures.
They set off with a team of explorers on an exciting expedition to the South Pole.
Then, halfway through the journey, Ponko and Joey fall off their sledge.
How will they ever reach the South Pole now? Based on a real toy penguin
that belonged to the famous Antarctic photographer, Herbert Ponting, this is a perfect story
for young children who are just beginning to explore their own worlds.
"Clear and delightful illustrations and empathetic vocabulary… children will
be fascinated by the link to the real toy."   *Geographical Association*

ISBN 1-84507-016-X

Honey Biscuits
Honey Cookies (USA)

Illustrated by Alison Bartlett

One cow? A thousand buzzing bees? The bark from a tree?
When Ben learns how to make cookies with his gran, he doesn't just find out how
to bake biscuits, he also discovers where all the ingredients come
from and whose help he really needs.
"This is my favourite children's cook book."   Sophie Grigson, *The Guardian*

ISBN 1-84507-045-3 (UK)
ISBN 1-84507-395-9 (USA)

Frances Lincoln titles are available from all good bookshops.
You can also buy books and find out more about your favourite titles,
authors and illustrators on our website: www.franceslincoln.com